# Who am I?

illustrated by
Normand Chartier

A GOLDEN BOOK, New York
Western Publishing Company, Inc.
Racine, Wisconsin 53404

Published by Western Publishing Company, Inc., in conjunction with Children's Television Workshop. Copyright © 178 Children's Television Workshop. Muppet characters copyright © 1971, 1972, 1973, 1974, 1978 Muppets, Inc. All rights reserved. Printed in the U.S.A. No part of this book may be reproduced or copied in any form without written permission from the publisher. GOLDEN®, GOLDEN® & DESIGN, A GOLDEN STURDY BOOK® and A GOLDEN BOOK® are trademarks of Western Publishing Company, Inc. ®Sesame Street and the Sesame Street sign are trademarks of Children's Television Workshop. Library of Congress Catalog Card Number: 78-55065

ISBN 0-307-62124-3

Who am I? I sleep in this room.
That is my old buddy, Bert.
And this is my very own Rubber Duckie.
I bet you can't guess who I am.

3

# Ernie.

Me have round, googly eyes.
Me have blue and shaggy fur.
Me always say, "Gimme cookie!"
What my name?

# Me Cookie Monster!

I live on Sesame Street
in a trash can.
That's because I *love* trash!
Guess who I am. Then
go away and leave me alone.

I'm Oscar the Grouch.

Greetings, and welcome to
my castle. I love to count
all of these wonderful things.
Who am I?

The Count.

Hello, everybodeee! I love to help
my friends on Sesame Street.
I am cute, adorable old . . .

13

. . .Grover.

14

# A Poem
## by (Guess Who)

I am big, I am yellow.
I am a feathery fellow.

I live in a nest, not in a cage.
Do you know who I am?
Please turn the page.

Big Bird.

I am big and brown, and I have a long snuffle. I am looking for my best friend, Bird. Oh dear, it's time for my nap. Do you know who I am?

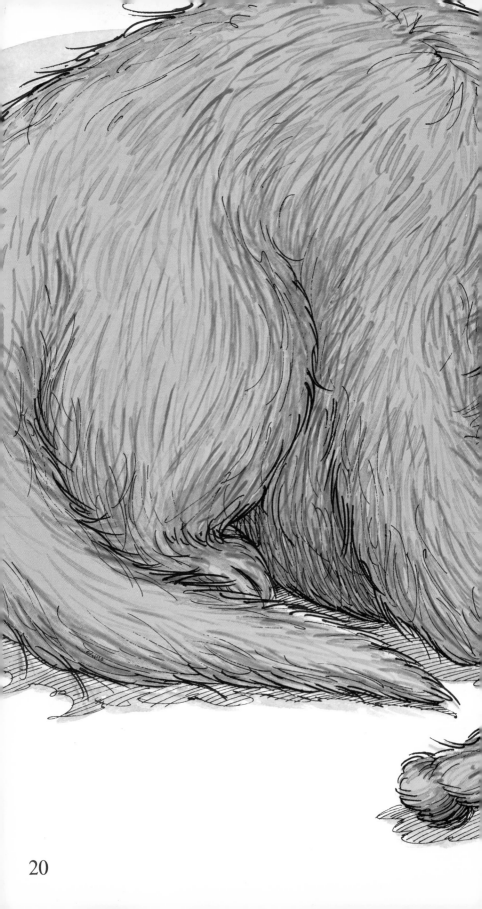

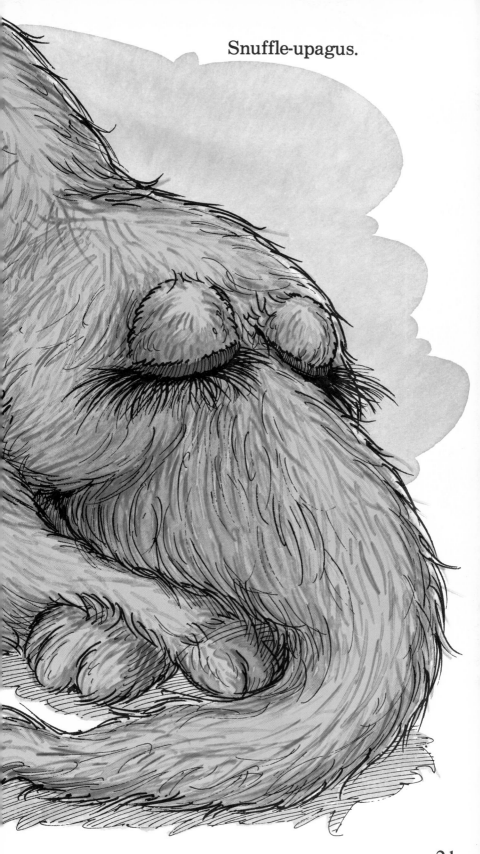

Snuffle-upagus.

This educational product was created in cooperation with the Children's Television Workshop, producers of "Sesame Street." Children do not have to watch the television show to benefit from this book. Workshop revenues from this product will be used to help support CTW educational projects.